There once was a forest, far out in the west.
A forest far greener, more lush than the rest.
Where in the calm mornings, soggy and damp,
One hears the birds chirping and the howl of a tramp.
The trees, they are tall, and thick at the trunk,
It smells like fresh rain and the stench of a skunk.

In this wet forest, as nice as a pearl,
There once lived a creature named Earl the Squirrel.
He lived deep in the woods, in a hollowed out log,
Where he was so hungry, he could eat a whole hog.
With winter approaching, there was no time to waste,
Earl must find him some acorns to satisfy his taste.

He searched all the bushes, the trees and the ground,
But despite all his efforts, no acorns were found.
He looked in the lake, then stared at the sun.
He climbed up the mountain, but still he found none.

With no acorns in his tummy, and none in his grasp,
He had an idea, and let out a small gasp.
Although of the acorns, himself he had none,
There were other squirrels who had way more than one.

It would be far too hard and too awkward to ask,
So instead Earl the Squirrel went and got a black mask.
With his black mask secure and a bag that was empty,
He set off to steal from the squirrels who had plenty.

He started that evening, the air cool and clear,
And began taking acorns without any fear.
He took not just one, not just two, not just three,
But instead enough acorns to fill a whole tree.

He stole them from Rachel, from Jon and from Zach,
He stole enough acorns to fill his whole sack.
He took them in handfuls, he stole a whole clump,
He continued to work 'til he heard a loud thump.

"Oh no!" Earl cried out. "Surely, I'm done!"
"Otto is coming! He's as fierce as the sun!"
Otto stormed out with a big kitchen pan.
Earl got so scared that he ran and he ran

Back at his log, now filled to the top,
Earl thought it was time to temporarily stop.
He ate and he ate, 'til he couldn't eat more,
Then fell into a slumber and started to snore.

Suddenly he awoke when his alarm clock went click!
It was then that he started to feel very sick.
His stomach was tight and his head felt quite warm,
And his throat felt like it had been hit by a storm.
A few hours went by of him feeling this way,
He thought, "This will not be a very good day."

He kept getting sicker and began to turn red.
The next thing he knew, he was in a strange bed.
He opened his eyes and took in the view.
His mother was there and Doctor Bill, too.
She asked, "Doctor, why is his stomach so big?"
The doc said, "It looks like he swallowed a pig!"

It took quite awhile until Earl did recover.
Feeling guilty, he finally confessed to his mother.
She told him to make right the wrong that he'd done,
"Just follow your heart and you'll be fine, my son."
Earl knew he could no longer deal with the shame,
So he said sorry to all, much too many to name.

He then went to work and gathered all day,
Every nut he could pick so that he could repay.
Then he vowed, "From this day on I won't steal a thing."
So they all joined together and started to sing.
And from that moment on, all was good, all was fair,
And the squirrels decided that they would just share.

Jacob (left)& Frankie (right)

About the Authors:

We are Jacob Warren and Frankie Cleary and we are seniors at Paradise High School. We are actively involved in both academics and athletics. We became friends early in elementary school through the local basketball league. Together, we wrote *Earl the Squirrel* during our junior year as an AP English assignment. We have published our written work as part of our Senior Project, a career or community service based project necessary to graduate from Paradise High School. Proceeds from our Senior Project will be used to provide local elementary school classes with copies of Earl the Squirrel.

Lightning Source UK Ltd.
Milton Keynes UK
UKRC020628150119
335575UK00005B/200